A catalogue record for this book is available from the British Library

Published by Ladybird Books Ltd Loughborough Leicestershire UK

Ladybird Books Ltd is a subsidiary of the Penguin Group of companies

Finnigan's Flap

by *Joan Stimson*
illustrated by Jacqueline East

Picture
Ladybird

Finnigan was fed up. He could never come and go as he pleased. On starry nights, Finnigan longed to slip out of the house and explore. On showery days, he wanted to nip back in when it rained. Sometimes he felt like a nap by the fire. Often he fancied a snack. What Finnigan needed was a cat flap.

But Finnigan lived with the Billings. And the Billings had a busy building business. They had two busy children as well, so although Finnigan was fed and loved and played with, no one had noticed how much he needed a cat flap.

Over the fence from Finnigan lived a cat called Selina. Now Selina had a *brilliant* cat flap.

And whenever Finnigan was shut out of *his* house, it was frustrating to see Selina — *SWISH*, *SWOOSH* — flip through the flap into *hers*.

It was worse when Finnigan was shut *in*.
Because then you could bet your last
cat biscuit that — *SWISH*, *SWOOSH* — Selina
would swan outside with her nose in the air.

Finnigan did his best to explain to the Billings.
He mewed and he squeaked and he showed
them the door where he wanted his flap. But
the Billings hadn't a clue.

"I'm doomed to be flapless!" wailed Finnigan to himself. And he tried not to notice as – *SWISH*, *SWOOSH* – Selina came and went as she pleased.

One morning the Billings were busier than
ever. But their van wouldn't start. Mr Billing
hunted for the handbook. Mrs Billing tore
open the tool kit. Billy Billing sprayed the
START spray, and Becky bawled instructions.

When at last the van leapt to life, there was a loud cheer. Apparently the Billings couldn't *bear* to be vanless. And suddenly, Finnigan knew the answer to his problem.

"All I have to do," he told himself, "is to show the Billings that *they* need a cat flap as much as *I* do!"

That evening Finnigan came in as soon as he was called. He curled up on his bed as quiet as a mouse.

But at midnight, *BOING, BOING, BOING!*
Finnigan danced on the piano keyboard and
asked to go out.

Next he squeezed through the window of the
Billings' van. *TOOOOOOOOOOOT!* He leant
on the horn until the Billings let him in again.

Soon the Billings were up and down like yo-yos.

Back in the house, Finnigan tucked his head
under a tea towel and crept upstairs.

"*EEEEEEEEK!*" Finnigan made a terrific ghost.

Finnigan was sent outside but found he could reach the doorbell. *DING DONG*, *DING DONG*, *DING DONG*, *DING DONGGGGGGGGGGG!* The Billings *soon* let him in again!

By now, the Billings were exhausted. Even Finnigan was beginning to flag. But... *BANG!* He still managed to burst the birthday balloons in the hall. And this time the Billings exploded, too.

Finnigan ran round to ring the doorbell again.
But then he decided against it. "I expect
they've got the message by now," he told
himself, "and anyway, they'll feel better after
a cat nap."

So, for the little that was left of the night,
Finnigan slept outside.

Next day the Billings went early-morning shopping. Eight busy hands all set to work at once.

And soon Something New and Exciting was ready to be tested!

Finnigan took to his flap like a duck to water.
At last he felt in charge of his nine lives.

And every single time he swanned in or out –
SWISH, SWOOSH – Finnigan felt *FANTASTIC!*

Finnigan's Flap Game

Here is a picture of Finnigan's neighbourhood. Look at the picture clues and see if you can find them in the main picture.

You will need to look very carefully – they are not easy to see!

Trowel

Ball

Bird

Selina

Dog

Bone

Finnigan

Duck

Mum

Billy

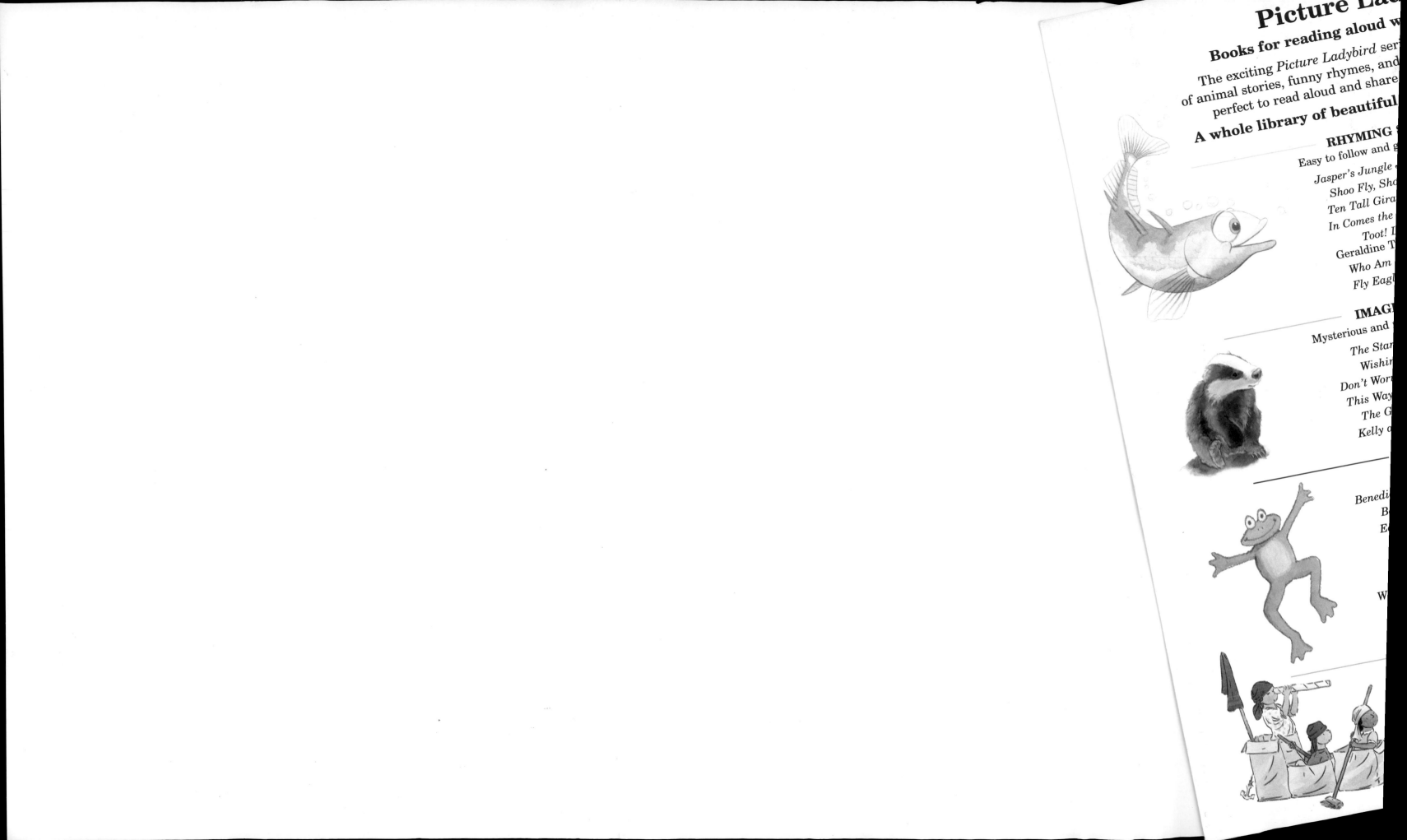